The Conjuring Wizard

Wizard

and Snippitty's Shears

illustrated by
Rene Cloke

AWARD PUBLICATIONS LIMITED

The Conjuring Wizard

Jimmy was dreadfully disappointed. He had been asked to a party that day, and now here he was in bed with a cold! It really was too bad.

Mummy was very sorry for him. 'Cheer up, darling,' she said. 'There will be lots more parties.'

'Yes, but this one is going to have a conjurer,' said Jimmy. 'Just think of that, Mummy! Oh, I do wish I was going to see him.'

Mummy looked so sad to think that he was in bed, that Jimmy made up his mind to be cheerful about the party, and to pretend he didn't really mind. So he lay in bed smiling, and tried not to mind when he heard the children arriving at the party next door.

Mummy brought him his tea, and when he had finished it he lay back in bed, half asleep. Suddenly he heard a knock at the door, and he called out: 'Come in!' thinking that perhaps it was Jane, the maid.

But it wasn't. It was a strange-looking man in a high, pointed hat. He wore a cloak, and on it were stars and half-moons.

'Good evening,' he said to the sur-
prised little boy. 'I heard you were not
very well, so I came along to see you. Do
you feel very dull?'

'It is a bit dull lying in bed with a cold
when you know there's a party next door
with a conjurer,' said Jimmy.

'A conjurer!' said the man. 'Do you like
conjurers?'

'I should just think I do!' said Jimmy.
'Why, at a party I went to last year there
was a conjurer who made some goldfish
come out of a silk handkerchief and swim
in a glass of water. And there was nothing

The Conjuring Wizard

in that handkerchief, because it was mine that I had had clean for the party!'

'Pooh, that's nothing!' said the strange-looking man. 'I can make goldfish come out of the pocket of your pyjamas and swim in your tea-cup!'

'You couldn't!' said Jimmy.

'Well, look here, then!' said the man, and he suddenly put his hand into Jimmy's pocket, took out three wriggly goldfish and popped them into the little boy's tea-cup, which suddenly became full of water. The fish swam about gaily, then leapt up into the air and vanished.

'Ooh!' said Jimmy, astonished. 'How did you do that?'

The Conjuring Wizard

'Aha!' said the man. 'I can do much cleverer things than that!'

'Then you must be a wizard,' said Jimmy. 'Perhaps I am,' said the man with a laugh. 'Just give me your handkerchief, will you?'

Jimmy gave it to him. The wizard folded it neatly into four and laid it on the bed.

The Conjuring Wizard

'There's nothing in it, is there?' he said to Jimmy. 'Just feel and see.'

Jimmy felt. No, the handkerchief was quite soft and flat. The wizard picked it up and shook it out with a laugh. Out ran a white rabbit – and another – and another – and another!

'Goodness!' gasped Jimmy, amazed. 'However did they get there? Ooh, look at them running all over the room!'

The rabbits ran here and there, and suddenly popped up the chimney.

'They have gone,' said the conjurer. 'Now I'll do another trick. Open your mouth Jimmy.'

The Conjuring Wizard

Jimmy opened it, and to his great surprise the wizard began to pull coloured paper out of it. More and more he pulled, till the bed was full of it. Jimmy shut his mouth at last, and looked at the paper in astonishment.

'Well!' he said, 'I can't think how my mouth held all that, really I can't. Do another trick, Mr. Conjurer.'

'I'll make the poker and shovel do a dance together,' said the conjurer. He waved his hands, and suddenly the poker and the shovel each grew two spindly legs and two thin arms. Then they began to

dance. How funny it was to see them! They bowed and kicked, jumped and sprang, and Jimmy laughed till tears came into his eyes.

'Now do another trick,' he said.

Then the wizard did a strange thing.
He picked up the coal-scuttle and emp-
tied all the coal on the bed!

'Oh, you mustn't do that,' said Jimmy.
'Mummy will be cross!'

'It's all right!' said the conjurer. 'Did
you think it was coal! Well, it's not!'

And to Jimmy's great astonishment he
saw that the lumps of coal had all turned
into toys! There was a fine clockwork
engine, a ship with a sail, a picture book,
a box of soldiers and an aeroplane.

'Good gracious!' cried Jimmy, 'What
fun!'

The wizard waved his hands once more. The engine leapt off the bed and ran round the floor. The ship jumped into Jimmy's wash-basin and sailed there. The soldiers sprang out of their box and marched up and down the bed in a line. The aeroplane flew round and round in the air, and the book began to read the stories aloud!

'You are a marvellous man!' cried Jimmy. 'Do tell me who you are and where you come from.'

The Conjuring Wizard

'Very well,' said the conjurer, and he sat down in the chair by Jimmy's bed. 'My name is . . .'

But just at that very minute there came another knock at Jimmy's door. The conjurer straightaway jumped through the window and vanished. The toys flew into the coal-scuttle and became coal, and the coloured paper shrivelled up and disappeared in the twinkling of an eye.

The Conjuring Wizard

The door opened and the doctor came in with Mummy.

'Hallo, hallo,' he said. 'And how are we feeling now?'

'He's looking better,' said Mummy. 'Why, Jimmy, you look quite excited. Anyone would think you had been seeing the conjurer after all!'

'And so I have!' said Jimmy. Then he told the Doctor and Mummy all about the marvellous wizard. But they didn't believe him at all. And then Jimmy suddenly saw one of the rabbits! It came popping down the chimney and jumped up on the bed.

The Conjuring Wizard

'You must believe me now, Mummy!' he said, 'For look, here's one of the rabbits!'

Jimmy still has that rabbit. Isn't he lucky?

Snippitty's Shears

Snippitty's garden was in a dreadful mess. The grass wanted cutting, the hedge wanted clipping, and the weeds had grown so tall that Snippitty could hardly see the flowers.

He had been away on his holiday, and he was very cross to see how untidy his garden was.

'I don't feel like spending all the week clipping and cutting,' he thought. 'I think

I'll go to Puddle the gnome and buy a pair of magic shears. Then they can do the work, and I shall be able to sit in the sunshine and read my newspaper.'

Snippitty's Shears

So he went to Puddle's shop. It was a curious shop, hung with all kinds of things, from pins to balloons. Puddle was very clever, and he could put a spell into anything and make it very powerful indeed.

'I want a pair of shears with a cutting spell in them,' said Snippitty, when he walked inside the shop.

'Here's a fine pair,' said Puddle, taking down a glittering pair of sharp-looking shears.

'How much?' asked Snippitty.

'Thirty pence,' said Puddle.

'Don't be foolish,' said Snippitty. 'That's far too much.'

'It isn't, and you know it isn't,' said Puddle indignantly. 'Why, you couldn't buy these shears at even fifty pence in the next town. They would be quite seventy pence.'

Snippitty knew that that was true. Puddle's shears were very good indeed, and the magic in them made them powerful.

Snippitty's Shears

But he was a mean little fellow, and he wasn't going to pay more than he could help.

'I'll give you twenty pence for them,' he said, getting out his purse.

'No,' said Puddle.

'Yes,' said Snippitty. 'Not a penny more.'

'No, I tell you,' said Puddle. 'Why, they cost more than that to make.'

'I don't believe you,' said Snippitty, rudely.

Puddle looked at the mean little gnome and felt very angry.

'All right,' he said suddenly, with a grin. 'You can have them for twenty pence.'

Snippitty smiled in delight to think that he had got his way. He paid out the money, took the shears and went off with them.

He stuck them in the grass and said loudly: 'Shears, do your work!'

At once the shears began cutting the grass very closely and evenly. Snippitty watched them, pleased to think that he could sit down and read whilst his shears did all his work.

When the shears had finished cutting his lawn, Snippitty saw them fly across to the privet hedge and begin to clip that.

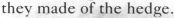

He was delighted to see what a fine job
they made of the hedge.

'I'll just finish this story in my paper
and then set the shears to work on those
tall weeds,' said Snippitty. So he settled
down comfortably to his reading – but,
dear me, his chair was so soft and the sun
was so warm that Snippitty fell fast
asleep!

He slept on and on – and the shears
went on and on working. They finished
the hedge and looked round for some-

thing else to clip. They flew across to the weeds and cut those down too. Then they clipped down all the rose trees that Snippitty was so proud of, and looked round for something else.

Clip! The clothes-line was cut in half and all the clothes fell to the ground. The shears soon cut them up into little pieces, and then looked round again.

Clip! Down came the tennis net, and was soon cut into tiny little pieces on the lawn. What next? Ha, there was Snippitty lying fast asleep in the sunshine, his long white beard reaching almost down to his knees.

The shears flew over to him. Clip! Clip! Clip! The beard that Snippitty was so proud of was cut into three pieces, and the shears began to clip it very small. The noise woke Snippitty, and he sat up and yawned.

Snippitty's Shears

But, oh, my goodness, when he saw what the shears had done, he shouted in dismay.

'Stop! Stop! Oh, you wicked shears, look what you've done! You've taken off my beautiful beard! You've chopped my clothes-line in half! You've cut down my rose trees! You've ruined my tennis net! Oh, oh, stop, I tell you, stop!'

But nothing would stop those shears! They rushed at Snippitty and cut off the points of his shoes. Then they snipped all the buttons off his tunic and clipped the point off his hat. Snippitty gave a yell and rushed up the road to Puddle's shop. He burst in at the door and closed it behind him.

Snippitty's Shears

'Good gracious, Snippitty, whatever's the matter?' asked Puddle.

'It's those shears!' said Snippitty, almost crying. 'They've got a spell to make them work, but not one to make them stop. Put it in at once, Puddle. Look what they've done to my lovely beard!'

Puddle laughed till the tears rolled down his long nose and dropped on the counter with a splash.

'If you want another spell, it will be ten pence extra,' he said. 'I told you those shears were thirty pence, you know. You only paid me twenty pence and surely you didn't expect to get such a lot for your money. Will you pay me ten pence more, and I will put a stop-spell in the shears?'

Snippitty opened his purse and put ten pence on the counter.

'I have been mean,' he said. 'And I am well punished. Here is your money. Take it.'

Snippitty's Shears

Puddle took it, and then opened the door. The shears flew in and Puddle chanted some magic words. At once the shears fell to the counter and lay there quite still.

Snippitty picked them up and shook them.

'You wicked things!' he cried. 'You've done pounds worth of damage! I'll put you in the dustbin!'

'Don't do that,' said Puddle. 'They might come in useful next year.'

'So they might,' said Snippitty, with a sigh and put them under his arm. 'Well, I'm going back to clear up all the damage. Good-day to you, Puddle. I shan't be mean again. It certainly doesn't pay.'

And I quite agree with him, don't you?

ISBN 0-86163-733-X

Text copyright Darrell Waters Limited
Illustrations copyright © 1994 Award Publications Limited

Enid Blyton's signature is a trademark of Darrell Waters Limited

First published in The Conjuring Wizard and other stories

This edition first published 1994 by Award Publications Limited,
Goodyear House, 52-56 Osnaburgh Street, London NW1 3NS

Printed in Italy